![DANIEL TIGER'S NEIGHBORHOOD]

Daniel and the Firefighters

Adapted by Alexandra Cassel Schwartz

Based on the screenplays "Firefighters at School" written by Eric Saiet and Andrea Scully and "Daniel's Doll" written by Jennifer Hamburg

Poses and layouts by Jason Fruchter

Simon Spotlight

New York London Toronto Sydney New Delhi

SIMON SPOTLIGHT
An imprint of Simon & Schuster Children's Publishing Division
1230 Avenue of the Americas, New York, New York 10020
This Simon Spotlight paperback edition December 2020
© 2020 The Fred Rogers Company
All rights reserved, including the right of reproduction in whole or in part in any form.
SIMON SPOTLIGHT and colophon are registered trademarks of Simon & Schuster, Inc.
For information about special discounts for bulk purchases, please contact Simon & Schuster Special Sales at 1-866-506-1949 or business@simonandschuster.com.
Manufactured in the United States of America 0521 LAK
10 9 8 7 6 5 4 3
ISBN 978-1-5344-8067-4
ISBN 978-1-5344-8068-1 (eBook)

It was a beautiful day in the neighborhood, and Daniel was at school.

"Guess who's visiting our class today?" Daniel said. "I'll give you a hint. They ride big, red trucks that go '*DING DING*' or '*WEE-OO! WEE-OO!*'"

"The neighborhood firefighters are coming!" Daniel cheered. He was excited to meet a real firefighter.

Daniel was pretending that a stuffie was a fire hose and was using it to put out a pretend fire. "*Whooosh!* Firefighter Daniel is here to help!" he said.

"Wow! You really do look like a firefighter, Daniel," Miss Elaina said.

"And you look like an astronaut!" Daniel told her.

Miss Elaina zoomed around, pretending the classroom was outer space.

Then Miss Elaina took off her astronaut helmet. *"WEE-OO! WEE-OO!"* she called out. "Firefighter Miss Elaina comin' through."

Daniel was confused. "You can't be a firefighter," he told Miss Elaina.

"Why not?" Miss Elaina asked, frowning.

"Because I thought you were an astronaut," Daniel said. "You're always an astronaut."

Miss Elaina shrugged. "I like to be different things," she explained. Teacher Harriet said, "It's true. Sometimes Miss Elaina may want to be an astronaut. Other times, she may want to be a firefighter, or even something else!" Then Teacher Harriet sang:

 "You can be more than one thing!"

Even Trolley was more than one thing! Fire Truck Trolley and the neighborhood firefighters arrived at the school for a special visit!

Daniel saw Music Man Stan! "Why is your dad wearing a firefighter's hat?" Daniel asked Miss Elaina. "I thought he worked at the Music Shop!"

Miss Elaina explained, "He does! He's also a firefighter . . . and a daddy!" Then she sang,

 "You can be more than one thing!"

Dr. Anna was a firefighter too! The class learned what it was like to be a real firefighter.

"When we hear there's a fire, we have to be fast!" Dr. Anna explained. "We put on these coats and hats to protect our bodies."

The firefighters passed out helmets for the kids to wear. Miss Elaina tried on a firefighter coat. "Whoa, that's heavy!" she said.

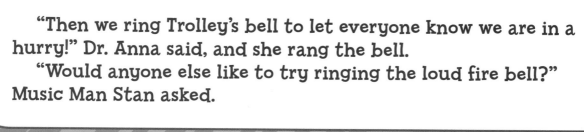

"Then we ring Trolley's bell to let everyone know we are in a hurry!" Dr. Anna said, and she rang the bell.

"Would anyone else like to try ringing the loud fire bell?" Music Man Stan asked.

"Ooh! Ooh! Me! Me!" Prince Wednesday said, running over. He was so excited that he accidentally tripped and scraped his hand. Luckily, Dr. Anna took care of him.

Prince Wednesday asked Dr. Anna, "Even though you're a firefighter now, are you still a doctor?"

"Of course," Dr. Anna said. "You can be more than one thing! I like to help people in different ways."

Daniel thought about what it would be like to be a *real* firefighter when he grew up! He had fun holding the fire hose . . . but there were other things he wanted to do too.

Daniel also loved soccer and taking care of his baby sister. "Hmm," he said. "I want to be a soccer-player-firefighter-daddy when I grow up!"

That gave Daniel an idea. He imagined all the things he could be when he grew up. He sang,

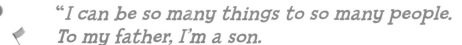

"I can be so many things to so many people.
To my father, I'm a son.
To Grandpere, I'm a grandson.
To my sister, I'm a brother.
And I'm a neighbor and a friend to everyone!

"I can be so many things in my imagination—
an Adventure Tiger or a dad.
I might be a famous painter or sail the seven seas,
or be a doctor or a fireman."

At the end of the day, Prince Tuesday came to pick up his little brother from school. He was wearing his lifeguard uniform.

"Wow!" Daniel said. "Prince Tuesday is *a lot* of things! Sometimes he's a waiter, sometimes he's a babysitter, and sometimes he's a lifeguard!"

"And I'm a brother, a son, and a neighbor, too!" Prince Tuesday added.

"You really *can* be more than one thing!" Daniel said.

"What do *you* want to be?" Daniel wanted to know. "There are so many things you can be! Ugga Mugga."